Ducklings

Kate Petty

BARRON'S

The nest

The mother duck searches for a safe and secret place to lay her eggs. She builds a nest with leaves and grass and lines it with her own downy breast feathers. She lays the first egg exactly four weeks after mating. Each day for the next eight days or so she lays another egg. Then she settles down to keep them warm for a month.

This mother duck is a Widgeon.

Duck eggs in the nest ▷

Out of the egg

About a month after the eggs were laid the ducklings are ready to chip their way out. This is hard work for a tiny duckling and it takes several hours. The duckling saws around the shell with its beak and pushes the two halves apart. Then it has to kick itself free. The newly hatched duckling is wet all over and rather shaky after its efforts.

Inside the eggs the ducklings are chipping at the shell.

The duckling's head emerges first. ▷

A new world

Soon all the ducklings have hatched. The mother duck helps to clear away each bit of shell. As their feathers dry out the ducklings start to look very fluffy and sweet, with shining eyes and big, flappy webbed feet. Inside the eggs the ducklings lived off the nutritious egg yolk. Now they are ready to find their first meal for themselves.

A Mallard duckling finally frees itself from the shell.

Day-old Mallards ▷

First swim

Ducklings naturally follow the first creature they see. So when their mother gently pushes them out of the nest and heads for the water, they have no choice but to follow her. Walking is difficult for them at first, but paddling along at their mother's side is really quite easy. Once back on the bank they shake the water from their feathers to dry off.

The ducklings take to the water without any trouble.

A duckling dries off after its swim. ▷

The duck family

Although the mother duck spent several months with the drake, or father duck, before her eggs hatched, she brings the ducklings up on her own. She keeps them warm in the nest and stays close when they are out of it. They follow her around in a long line and she does her best to protect them from hungry predators.

These are Barrow's Goldeneye ducks.

Ducklings stay close to their mother. ▷

Eating

Ducklings have to feed themselves as soon as they hatch. They copy their mother as she snaps at little insects hovering close to the water. As they grow older they learn to up-end themselves and dive for creatures below the surface. They eat water weeds too. At night ducks go on land and find berries, seeds and worms to eat, as other birds do.

It takes time for ducklings to learn how to dive.

Ducks feeding on land ▷

Learning to fly

The little ducklings cannot learn to fly until their feathers grow longer and their wing muscles strengthen. At first, they just hop into the air and float to the ground. They have to learn to take off by flapping their wings strongly. Once the ducklings can fly the mother no longer needs to protect them.

These are Spectacled Eider.

Ducks can take off and land in water. ▷

Fine feathers

Ducklings have to learn to take care of their feathers. Feathers keep them warm and dry in wet and cold weather. A duck cleans its feathers by combing through them with its bill. It makes them waterproof by spreading oil over them from the "preen gland" near its tail. Males, or drakes, have more brightly colored feathers than females.

Male and female Tufted Ducks

Duckling preening ▷

Ducktalk

By the autumn the ducklings are old enough to choose a mate for the following spring. The female ducks and male drakes show off to each other. The female stretches out her neck along the water and nods her head to show that she wants to find a mate. The drake pretends to preen and makes rattling noises, or he shakes water all around with a grunting, whistling sound.

A Pochard drake showing off to the female.

The female nods to the drake she has chosen. ▷

Taking off

As the weather grows colder the ducks fly to warmer places where they will find more food. The flock sets off in the evening and flies all night. They rest in the day and then fly on again until they arrive at a suitable place. After the winter many of the ducks return to where they hatched to raise their own families.

A flock of Lesser Scaup

Ruddy Shelducks flying in a V formation ▷

Duckling facts

There are many different kinds of ducks you might see in parks, on ponds or in wild places. Most ducks choose a partner in the autumn and mate in the following spring. The young ducklings hatch two months later. All breeds are fully grown by the time they are one year old. Some, like Mallards, are grown up and ready to choose a mate at six months.

Newborn

Adult female

Adult male

Index

Photgraphic credits:

Cover and pages 13, 17 and 21: Ardea;
pages 3, 9, 15 and 19: Frank Lane Agency;
pages 5, 7, and 11: Bruce Coleman.

Design	David West Children's Book Design
Illustrations	George Thompson
Picture Research	Cee Weston-Baker

First paperback edition for the United States
and Canada published 1993 by Barron's
Educational Series, Inc.

First published in the United States 1990 by
Gloucester Press.

© Copyright 1990 by Aladdin Books Ltd

All inquiries should be addressed to:
Barron's Educational Series, Inc.
250 Wireless Boulevard
Hauppauge, NY 11788

Library of Congress
Catalog Card No. 90-32398
International Standard
Book No. 0-8120-1489-8 (paperback)

Library of Congress Cataloging-in-Publication Data

Petty, Kate.
   Ducklings/ Kate Petty.
   p.cm.— (Baby animals)
   Summary: Describes how Ducklings
are hatched and fed, how they learn to
walk and fly, and how they communicate.
   ISBN 0-8120-1489-8 (paperback)
1. Ducks — Infancy Juvenile literature.
(Ducks 2. Animals — Infancy.) I. Title. II.
Series: Petty, Kate. Baby animals.
QL 696.A52P44 1990
598.4'1—dc20   90-32398
                                            CIP AC

PRINTED IN BELGIUM

3456   987654321